The Bitty Twins
On the Go

Written by Jennifer Hirsch
Illustrated by Renate Lohmann

We're going to the park
to spend the day outside.

Let's get into our stroller
and take a little ride.

So many cars and trucks!
What's that ahead of us,

with people getting on and off?
It's a great big . . .

. . . bus!

We're stopping at the lake.
It's lots of fun to float,
sitting on the water
in a paddleboat.

Hey, look at all those ducklings!
I saw a frog—did you?
I see a long and narrow boat.
It must be a . . .

. . . canoe!

Riding through the park,
pedaling our trikes,

we like to wave at people
riding bigger bikes.

What's that noisy rumble? Do you think it's going to rain?

The rumble
sounds like
thunder, but it
isn't—it's a . . .

. . . train!

That was quite a ride,
the best that we've had yet.

Are you two ready to go home?

No, we're not! Not yet!

Shall we go for one more ride?

Another ride—hurray!

How 'bout
in a rocket?

Or maybe
in a sleigh!

You can't ride in a sleigh
unless the weather's snowing.

I forgot. Oh well!
I wonder where we're going?

So many ways to travel—
by stroller, trike, or train,
by bus, canoe, or paddleboat,
or walking with a cane!
Which way do we like best?
If you really want to know . . .

. . . I think this horse and carriage
is our favorite way to go!

Dear Parents . . .

Children love to ride on things! There's an excitement associated with motion and mobility that delights children of all ages. These travel games will help your child learn about different vehicles and safety features—and help keep her occupied on long trips.

A Special Outing

If you and your child usually drive places, make an outing or errand special by taking the bus. The trip will take a bit longer, but you'll be free of the distraction of driving and can use the time to have fun with your child. What do you see out the window? Try games like spotting red cars or counting all the trucks. Don't forget to wave at other buses!

Things You Can Ride On

On a family car trip, see how many different "things you can ride on" everyone can think of. To get the ideas flowing, offer hints such as "What animals can you ride on?" or "What do people ride on in the snow?" Older children will enjoy thinking up exotic answers like "a unicycle" or "a magic carpet."

Safety Matchup

Help your child draw lines to match each safety feature to the ride with which it is used:

helmet

car

car seat

boat

life vest

trike

Are We There Yet?

Before a long trip, give your child a small bag of tickets (colored paper rectangles). Explain that the trip will take three hours, and every half hour, you'll tell her to give you a ticket. When she's down to her last ticket, she'll know that means the trip is almost over! Young children love the ritual of handing over tickets, and after they've played this game a few times, they develop a feel for how much longer "two more tickets" is.

For a lengthy car or plane trip, prepare a series of little surprise packages containing a small toy or a fun food, such as a fruit roll-up or miniature box of cereal. The mini presents will help keep your little one occupied—and give her something to look forward to besides the end of the trip.